# The Toilet Paper Caper of 2020

# The Toilet Paper Caper of

## Mark H. McCraw

PALMETTO
PUBLISHING

Charleston, SC
www.PalmettoPublishing.com

*The Toilet Paper Caper of 2020*
Copyright © 2022 by Mark H. McCraw



Permission to use material from other works: www.istockphoto.com
Credits for illustrations or photos: www.istockphoto.com
Credits for cover design: www.fiverr.com (amy_creative) Freelance Project Book Cover Designer
Edited by: Freelance Professional Writers and Editors from www.fiverr.com (belovedmide) and (trentond)

Printed in the United States of America.
For more information or requests, please email the author at worldprofessor1@gmail.com.

First Edition

Hardcover ISBN: 979-8-9858936-0-1
Paperback ISBN: 979-8-9858936-1-8
eBook ISBN: 979-8-9858936-2-5

*This book is dedicated to
my grandson John.*

In the year 2020,
toilet paper was not aplenty.

Stores seemed
to run out.
I could not
understand
what it was
all about.

2

My mom said it was so funny...

when some stores raised the prices and
other people sold it

for more money.

I believed a fairy made it disappear ...

something that we use for our rear.

All because of a year of disease,

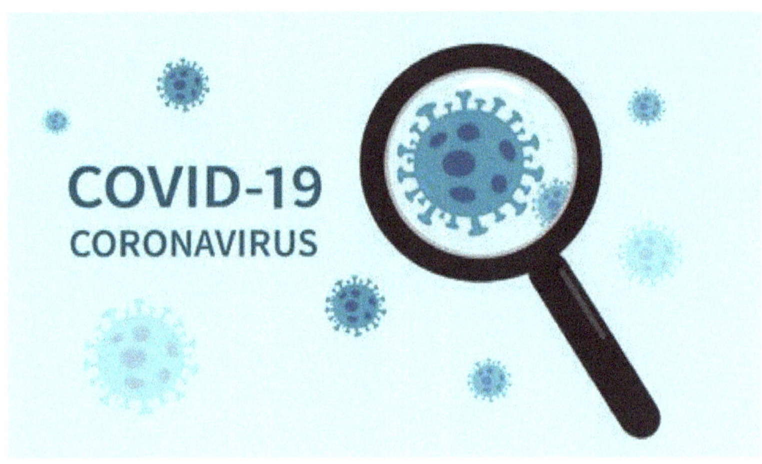


I ran out of toilet paper.

I need some more please.

So, my dad went to the store,
but there was no more.
There always used to be toilet
paper before.
I looked around high and low.

But I did not know...
why the stores were so low.

So, I got mad
because I felt like I had been had...

# Over the biggest caper...

that made the headlines of the paper.

So, I asked my mom
why the workers were so lazy
but she said the world had gone crazy.

# This was the year that was so hazy...

...all over the
biggest roll...

...that took a toll

on me having to do without.
So, I figure it was not good to pout.
So, I just tried to figure out
what was the deal

...when people were buying toilet paper like it was their last meal.

I am glad I finally have it.

Now, I try to conserve every bit.

# Afterward

The year 2020 had many challenges. One of them was that toilet paper was disappearing from the store shelves. People were stocking up on toilet paper even to the point of selling toilet paper, due to the shortage. Stores had to limit how many packages and rolls of toilet paper customers could get. Also, the stores could not keep the shelves stocked. That was the year of the COVID disease. This is the journey of a boy who is not too happy about not having toilet paper to use when he goes to the bathroom. He does not really know what COVID is—he just wants toilet paper. Naturally, his temper gets the best of him, but it all works out at the end.

Mark H. McCraw has spent more than a decade in education, working with children and students of all ages, from infants through college students. He is a father of four adult children and a grandfather of nine grandchildren. He currently lives in Oklahoma.